PLAYING

AMERICA'S

GAME

THE STORY OF
NEGRO LEAGUE BASEBALL

AN EARLY PHOTOGRAPH OF PHILADELPHIA'S HILLDALE CLUB
Afro-American Historical and Cultural Center, Philadelphia

PLAYING AMERICA'S GAME

THE STORY OF NEGRO LEAGUE BASEBALL

MICHAEL L. COOPER

LODESTAR BOOKS

DUTTON   NEW YORK

Library of Congress Cataloging-in-Publication Data
Cooper, Michael L.
Playing America's game: the story of Negro league baseball / Michael L. Cooper.
p. cm.
Includes bibliographical references and index.
Summary: A photo essay that presents the history of the Negro baseball leagues, a separate
version of baseball played in the first half of the twentieth century by those prevented because
of their race from playing in the major leagues.
ISBN 0-525-67407-1
1. Baseball—United States—History—Juvenile literature. 2. Afro-American baseball players—
Biography—Juvenile literature.
[1. Baseball—History. 2. Afro-Americans—Biography.] I. Title.
GV863.A1C615 1993
796.357′0973—dc20   92-2927
CIP
AC

Published in the United States by Lodestar Books,
an affiliate of Dutton Children's Books,
a division of Penguin Books USA Inc.,
375 Hudson Street, New York, New York 10014

Published simultaneously in Canada
by McClelland & Stewart, Toronto

Editor: Virginia Buckley   Designer: Katy Riegel
Printed in the U.S.A.   First Edition   10 9 8 7 6 5 4 3 2 1

TO
RICHARD C. SACHS

ACKNOWLEDGMENTS

Many people have devoted much time and energy researching and writing about the Negro leagues. Their groundwork has made this book possible. I would like to thank, in alphabetical order, Janet Bruce, Richard Clark, Craig Davidson, Lawrence D. Hogan, John B. Holway, Jerry Malloy, Luis Munoz, Buck O'Neil, Jim Riley, Donn Rogosin, Rob Ruck, and Morgan Smith.

Libraries, historical societies, and other institutions that preserve manuscripts and photographs are invaluable sources for writers and scholars. Unfortunately, severe budget cuts at all levels of government have curtailed or ended access to many archives. These cutbacks make the surviving institutions even more valuable. The following people and their organizations were particularly helpful in providing photographs and historical information about the Negro leagues: Charles L. Blockson, curator of the Blockson Afro-American Collection at Temple University; photo librarian Pat Kelly and her staff at the National Baseball Hall of Fame Library; Larry Lester, research director of the Negro Leagues Museum; the Schomburg Center for Research in Black Culture; and Rowenna Stuart and her staff at the Afro-American Museum in Philadelphia.

CONTENTS

THE PHOTOGRAPHIC RECORD OF BLACK ATHLETES

Professional athletes are among the most photographed people in the United States. But until the 1940s, with some exceptions such as heavyweight boxing champion Joe Louis and Olympic gold medalist Jesse Owens, black athletes were not popular subjects for photographers.

Blacks did not play in the top professional leagues in either baseball, football, or basketball. Thousands of blacks did play sports in high school and college as well as on all-black professional teams, but white-dominated newspapers and magazines rarely covered their accomplishments. Sports were important to black-owned newspapers such as the Chicago *Defender*, Pittsburgh *Courier*, and Baltimore *Afro-American*. These weeklies, however, lacked the resources to provide extensive coverage.

Individuals, frequently the athletes themselves, saved the photographs we have today. But many photos have been lost; others remain in private collections, especially as they become more valuable. Fortunately, in the last few years people have begun donating their collections to libraries and museums. Often these photographs are not dated nor are their subjects identified, but they are the beginnings of an important public record.

THE EAST TEAM AT THE 1939 EAST-WEST ALL-STAR CLASSIC,
WHICH ATTRACTED FORTY THOUSAND FANS. AS THEIR
UNIFORMS SHOW, THESE ALL-STARS REPRESENTED MANY
DIFFERENT TEAMS.
Refocus Films

1

THE DREAM GAME

THE EAST-WEST ALL-STAR CLASSIC

People called it the dream game. And what a dream. The East-West All-Star Classic was the world's biggest all-black sporting event. The best baseball players from the Negro leagues met every August at Chicago's Comiskey Park for one glorious, hard-fought game.

The all stars represented such legendary Negro league teams as the Kansas City Monarchs, Homestead Grays, Pittsburgh Crawfords, Chicago American Giants, Newark Eagles, New York Black Yankees, New York Cuban Stars, and Baltimore Elites. Every summer over a million fans voted for their favorite players. Those men selected from the East Coast staffed the East team, and those selected from the Midwest staffed the West team.

The annual East-West All-Star Classic began in 1933, and by the 1940s, the games packed as many as fifty thousand people into Comiskey Park. These fans came by car, bus, or train from as far away as New York, New Orleans, and Los Angeles. They traveled to Chicago to see baseball, but there

HENRY MILTON OF THE WEST COLLIDES AT HOME PLATE WITH
CATCHER JOSH GIBSON OF THE EAST IN THE 1939 GAME.
National Baseball Library, Cooperstown, N.Y.

was much more. Jazz musician Cab Calloway, Olympic gold-medal winner Jesse Owens, world heavyweight boxing champion Joe Louis, and other black celebrities always showed up. Chicago's prominent black citizens gave elaborate parties in their homes. And men and women in the many night clubs on Chicago's South Side swung to jazz and swayed to the blues.

Few white people attended the East-West games. In those days, whites and blacks played baseball on separate teams, in separate leagues. Whites played in the American League or the National League and capped their season with the World Series. Blacks played in the Negro leagues; their season's big event was the East-West All-Star Classic.

Fans filled Comiskey Park to see such players as Leroy "Satchel" Paige. His frequent pitching duels against top major leaguers made Paige the most famous Negro league player of the 1930s. His fastball, many people believe, was the fastest in baseball history. In the 1941 Classic, the West saved Paige for the last three innings. Taking the mound in the seventh,

SATCHEL PAIGE, THE NEGRO LEAGUE'S MOST FAMOUS
PITCHER, SHOWS OFF HIS WINDUP.
Negro Leagues Baseball Museum, Inc.

A DRAWING IN THE PITTSBURGH *COURIER* PROMOTES THE 1937 EAST-WEST
ALL-STAR CLASSIC. BLACK-OWNED NEWSPAPERS LIKE THE
COURIER CARRIED NEWS ABOUT BLACK BASEBALL TO HUNDREDS
OF THOUSANDS OF FANS IN ALL PARTS OF THE NATION.
Refocus Films

he fanned the first power hitter with straight strikes. On his
way to the plate, the next batter asked what Paige was pitching. "I don't know," the first batter replied. "I didn't see it."

In the 1945 East-West game, Jackie Robinson, a rookie
with the Kansas City Monarchs, played shortstop for the
West. He would soon be famous as the first black man in the
twentieth century to play major league baseball. But to people
in the stands at Comiskey, Robinson was practically unknown
compared to the East's Willie Wells. This Texas native was
playing his eighth Classic. Most fans thought Wells, a short-

stop for the Newark Eagles, was the leading infielder in black baseball. But he was only one of many exceptional athletes who appeared frequently in the annual game.

Outfielder James "Cool Papa" Bell played in seven East-West games. Possibly the fastest man in baseball, Bell reportedly ran the bases in twelve seconds flat!

Martín Dihigo, one of Cuba's greatest athletes and one of many Cuban ball players in the Negro leagues, played every position except catcher. In the 1935 East-West game, Dihigo started in center field and finished as pitcher.

Catcher Josh Gibson appeared in ten East-West All-Star Classics and often batted above .500. Fans frequently compared him to the famous major leaguers, Babe Ruth and Ty Cobb.

COOL PAPA BELL, ONE OF BASEBALL'S FASTEST BASE RUNNERS. HE WAS ELECTED TO THE NATIONAL BASEBALL HALL OF FAME IN 1974.
National Baseball Library, Cooperstown, N.Y.

IN THE LAST INNING OF THE 1935 EAST-WEST GAME, MULE
SUTTLES SLUGGED A DRAMATIC 475-FOOT HOME RUN TO GIVE
THE WEST A 11—8 VICTORY.
National Baseball Library, Cooperstown, N.Y.

Gibson and the other Negro league stars were more than outstanding baseball players. "Black athletes could only make a living playing black baseball," explained a manager for the Kansas City Monarchs. "You couldn't make it in basketball and football at the time. But in baseball you could make a living if you played year round. So what was happening was that the greatest black athletes in the world were playing black baseball."

These men symbolized black pride at a time when blacks were prevented from participating equally in American life. Forced to play a separate version of America's favorite sport, these talented athletes thrilled and delighted fans throughout the first half of the twentieth century.

2

NO BLACKS

BASEBALL DRAWS THE LINE

If he had a white face he would be playing with the best of them. . . . Those who know say there is no better second baseman in the country." That was a sportswriter's opinion of Bud Fowler, one of at least sixty black men who played minor and major league baseball in the latter half of the nineteenth century.

While complete statistics are not available for Fowler's career or for other black players of this era, those that do exist support this sportswriter's opinion of Fowler. In 1887 he played for the Binghamton Bingos in the International League. He batted .350 that season and stole twenty-three bases. In addition to being a skillful second baseman, Fowler was a versatile athlete who could pitch, catch, and play left field.

Another top player was Moses Fleetwood Walker. At Oberlin College in Ohio he was catcher on the school team. Walker began his professional career in 1883 with the Toledo Mud-

BUD FOWLER, IN THE MIDDLE OF THE BACK ROW, WAS ONE OF THE
TOP BLACK BASEBALL PLAYERS IN THE NINETEENTH CENTURY.
Jerry Malloy and Negro Leagues Baseball Museum, Inc.

hens. That season he caught in sixty games and helped the Mudhens win a pennant.

Perhaps the era's top black professional was Frank Grant. This second baseman played forty-five games in 1886 for the Buffalo Bisons. He batted .340, the team's highest average and the league's third highest average. The following year he led the league in batting and home runs. Grant "can fill creditably every position on the diamond," an enthusiastic sportswriter wrote. "He is exceedingly hard to fool at the bat . . . and his shots are generally long. . . . I think I can say that Grant is the best all-around player Buffalo ever had."

Despite their obvious skills, blacks in the white-dominated leagues suffered constant discrimination. Grant's teammates refused to pose with their leading batter for a club photograph. On Walker's team a white pitcher admitted, "He was the best catcher I ever worked with, but I disliked a Negro,

THIS CARTOON APPEARED IN A LEADING NATIONAL MAGAZINE IN THE 1880S. IT ILLUSTRATED THE WAY MANY WHITES VIEWED BLACK BASEBALL PLAYERS.
Dr. Lawrence D. Hogan

and whenever I had to pitch to him, I used anything I wanted without looking at his signals."

The International League announced in 1887 that "many of the best players in the league were eager to leave on account of the colored element. [The league] would approve no more contracts with colored men."

The last known black of the era to play in the majors was "Chief Tokohama." This second baseman masqueraded as an Indian to join the Baltimore Orioles. Indians, unlike blacks, could play in the majors. At a preseason game, knowing Chief Tokohama's real identity, proud black fans cheered so loudly that the opposing team's manager became suspicious. He later checked the second baseman's background and discovered that Tokohama was neither a chief nor an Indian. He was a black man named Charlie Grant. The Orioles promptly kicked Grant

CHARLIE GRANT PLAYED BRIEFLY IN THE MAJOR LEAGUES BY
PRETENDING TO BE AN AMERICAN INDIAN.
Refocus Films

SEGREGATION MEANT THAT BLACK PEOPLE AND WHITE PEOPLE
USED SEPARATE FACILITIES, SUCH AS WATER FOUNTAINS.
UPI/Bettmann

off the team. For nearly a half century afterward, major league and minor league baseball excluded blacks completely.

They were excluded because of growing white hostility toward black people. Most American blacks had been slaves until they were freed during the Civil War, which ended in 1865. But white people were never comfortable with the newly freed blacks. By 1900 numerous laws and customs segregated the two races in nearly every aspect of life. Blacks and whites rode in separate train cars, ate in separate restaurants, and were even buried in separate cemeteries.

THE ORIGINAL CUBAN GIANTS WERE NOT CUBANS. THEY WERE
BLACK AMERICANS WHO CALLED THEMSELVES CUBANS
BECAUSE DARK-SKINNED PEOPLE OF SPANISH DESCENT FACED
LESS DISCRIMINATION.
National Baseball Library, Cooperstown, N.Y.

Racism became so harsh that one of the first all-black base-ball teams called itself Cuban—the Cuban Giants. These players pretended they were Cubans because in the United States people of Spanish descent faced less discrimination than blacks. Organized in New York in 1885, the team barnstormed up and down the East Coast, winning an impressive number of games against semiprofessional and professional teams.

The Cuban Giants never lacked opponents. By the end of the century, baseball had become America's most popular sport, played by men and boys in every part of the country. Even the smallest towns fielded semiprofessional teams that competed against neighboring towns and barnstorming teams.

The best black teams were in Chicago, New York, Pittsburgh, Philadelphia, and other northern cities where the growing number of southern black migrants created large communities. These teams were black America's big leagues, and their players were among the most outstanding in baseball.

3

PLAYING THE GAME

EARLY YEARS AND STARS OF BLACK BASEBALL

Asked to name the world's greatest baseball player, one sportswriter replied that, of course, in the majors it was Babe Ruth. But in all of baseball, "the answer would have to be a colored man named John Henry Lloyd." Did this sportswriter know what he was talking about? A series of games in Cuba suggests he did.

After the season in the United States, many players sailed to Cuba. Baseball was a national passion on that tropical island. Teams there paid Americans handsomely to spend the winter playing the game amid palm trees and adoring fans. In 1910, Lloyd and several other black Americans joined one of Cuba's top teams, the Havana Reds. The Detroit Tigers, that year's World Series winner, visited the island for a series of games against Havana.

Eager Cubans filled the stadium to see Detroit's Ty Cobb. He led the American League that season in batting with an average of .385. Cobb, in fact, led the league in hitting eight

THE LINCOLN GIANTS IN 1915 IN PALM BEACH, FLORIDA. RESORT HOTELS
HIRED BLACK BASEBALL PLAYERS AS WAITERS. BETWEEN MEALS, THEY PLAYED
BASEBALL FOR THE ENTERTAINMENT OF WEALTHY GUESTS. JOHN HENRY LLOYD
IS IN THE TOP ROW, THIRD FROM THE LEFT.
Reid Poles and Negro Leagues Baseball Museum, Inc.

years straight. He was one of the greatest sluggers of all time.
In five games in Cuba he batted .371, not bad for fourth place.
Ahead of Cobb were three black Americans: Bruce Petway
batting .388, Grant "Home Run" Johnson .412, and Lloyd top-
ping the list with .500.

Lloyd returned to the United States the following spring
and joined the New York Lincoln Giants as shortstop. This
extraordinary team included center fielder Spotswood Poles,
left fielder Jimmy Lyons, and catcher Louis Santop. That year
the Lincoln Giants posted a 105–17 win-loss record with Poles,
Lyons, Santop, and Lloyd all batting above .400. Lloyd's ca-

AN EARLY PHOTOGRAPH OF PHILADELPHIA'S HILLDALE CLUB
Afro-American Historical and Cultural Center, Philadelphia

reer spanned a quarter of a century. He played for and managed the best black clubs of the era—the Lincoln Giants, the Chicago American Giants, and Philadelphia's Hilldale Club. Lloyd is one of only eleven Negro league players in the National Baseball Hall of Fame at Cooperstown, New York.

Another member of the Hall of Fame is Oscar Charleston. The center fielder astounded fans by his ability to chase down long fly balls. "Oscar was the only player I've ever seen," a teammate recalled, "who could turn twice while chasing a fly and then take it over his shoulder." In 1921, playing for the St. Louis Giants, Charleston batted .434, stole thirty-four bases, and led the new Negro National League in doubles and home runs. Years later, black sportswriters voted Charleston the greatest Negro league player of all time.

Many people like to compare Charleston, Lloyd, and other exceptional black athletes to the very best major league players such as Ty Cobb and Babe Ruth. But black players and teams differed from their major league counterparts in several ways that complicate comparisons. First of all, competition among the black squads was uneven. The Hilldale Club, for

OSCAR CHARLESTON, ONE OF THE ERA'S GREAT OUTFIELDERS,
PLAYED FOR SEVERAL TEAMS, INCLUDING RUBE FOSTER'S
CHICAGO AMERICAN GIANTS.
National Baseball Library, Cooperstown, N.Y.

example, might have faced the American League's Philadelphia Athletics in an exhibition game one day and the next day played a semiprofessional team of Pittsburgh steelworkers.

Also, since they were always struggling to make money, black teams squeezed as many games as possible into their schedules. Here's how one player remembered a very long day. "On Sunday in Philadelphia we'd go to the YMCA at five o'clock in the morning to change clothes. We'd get into uniform and go up into [New] Jersey and play a game at nine o'clock for some picnic or something. We'd leave from there and go to Dexter Park in Brooklyn and play the Bushwicks a doubleheader, and leave there and go out on Long Island and play a night game. It would be five o'clock the next morning when we'd get back to Philadelphia."

Black baseball also differed significantly from the majors in that players frequently changed clubs. Lloyd, for example, switched teams three times in four years, once in the middle of a season. Lloyd's explanation—"Wherever the money was, that's where I was."

Despite the differences, few people today doubt that Charleston, Lloyd, and other Negro league stars were as good as major league players. But in the early part of the twentieth century, many people believed black people were inferior to white people in every way. Blacks proved otherwise, especially when they faced major league teams in exhibition games.

"So as far as the competition, I could see no difference in the major leagues and our leagues, as far as hitting against the different pitchers," said Gene Benson, a Philadelphia Stars outfielder. "When we played head to head, it was nip and tuck. They won some and we won some. The white ball players knew it. They respected us. They considered us equals."

This equality upset some people. In the mid-1920s, baseball's first commissioner, Kenesaw Mountain Landis, ordered

American and National League teams to stop competing against black teams. Landis, many people believe, felt that losing to blacks embarrassed the major leagues. But postseason ball games were too popular and too profitable to give up. Major league players skirted the commissioner's order by organizing all-star teams, usually a mix of major and minor leaguers, to challenge the top black teams. One researcher found newspaper records of 167 games during the 1930s between all-star white teams and black teams, with blacks winning two-thirds of those contests.

"Smokey" Joe Williams compiled an impressive number of victories against major league squads. One of the most talked

SMOKEY JOE WILLIAMS' TREMENDOUS FASTBALL INSPIRED HIS NICKNAME.
National Baseball Library, Cooperstown, N.Y.

about duels of his long career occurred in 1915. Smokey Joe and the New York Lincoln Giants faced the National League champion Philadelphia Phillies. In the fourth inning, with the score 0–0 and no outs, the Phils loaded the bases. Smokey Joe, demonstrating his remarkable control, threw nine straight strikes. The Lincoln Giants beat the Phillies 1–0. Available statistics show that in a twenty-two-year career, Smokey Joe compiled a 19–7 record, including ten shutouts, against major league teams.

The big leagues discovered Smokey Joe, a six-and-a-half foot right-hander, in 1910. He was twenty-four-years old and pitching in Texas for the San Antonio Bronchos. Another native Texan and highly acclaimed pitcher recruited Smokey Joe. This was Andrew "Rube" Foster, perhaps the most important figure in black baseball.

4

THE FATHER OF BLACK BASEBALL

RUBE FOSTER AND THE NEGRO NATIONAL LEAGUE

Fans and players adored the big, friendly Texan. Rube Foster stood six feet, four inches and weighed over two hundred pounds. In his southern drawl he called everybody darlin' and enjoyed telling stories about rough-and-tumble Texas baseball. He earned the nickname Rube after hurling a winning game against the American League's Philadelphia Athletics and its famous pitcher Rube Waddell.

Like many black players, Foster began his baseball career early. In his mid-teens the tall, stout youth joined the Yellow Jackets, a semiprofessional team in Fort Worth, Texas. A couple of years later Foster moved north. He pitched for two Philadelphia squads from 1902 to 1906. Then the offer of a bigger paycheck persuaded him to join the Leland Giants in Chicago, where he was soon famous.

Foster, who had a persuasive manner and a keen eye for talent, talked several of his Philadelphia teammates into moving with him to Chicago. They included three power hitters:

THE PHILADELPHIA GIANTS IN 1905. GRANT "HOME RUN"
JOHNSON IS ON THE LEFT, TOP ROW. SECOND FROM THE LEFT
IS PITCHER RUBE FOSTER. CHARLIE GRANT IS IN THE TOP
ROW ON THE RIGHT. THE TEAM HAD ONLY TEN PLAYERS.
Refocus Films

John Henry Lloyd, Grant "Home Run" Johnson, and Pete
Hill. These newcomers made Chicago's Leland Giants nearly
unbeatable. In the 1907 season the Lelands won 110 of 120
games. In a postseason series against the City All Stars, a
pick-up team of major league and minor league players, Foster pitched and won four games.

Batters feared Foster's searing fastball and his "nasty
screwball thrown from a submarine delivery." His brilliance
on the mound impressed black fans and white fans alike. The
Chicago Cubs manager called Foster "the most finished prod-
uct I've ever seen in the pitcher's box." A sportswriter compared him to three outstanding major league pitchers. "Rube
Foster is a pitcher with the tricks of a Radbourne, with the

speed of a Rusie and with the coolness and deliberation of a Cy Young. What does that make him? Why, the greatest baseball pitcher in the country." While many people praised Foster's pitching, his influence extended far beyond the mound.

After three years with the Lelands, Foster organized his own club. He named it the Chicago American Giants. In its first season the new team won 123 games while losing only 6. Foster's Giants played half of their games barnstorming and the other half in the Chicago City League. This semiprofessional league included one other black team and a dozen all-white teams such as the Logan Squares and Duffy Florals. The American Giants captured the City League pennant three years in a row—1910, 1911, and 1912.

American Giants players were superior for several reasons. "Foster had little use for a man who could not bat from either side of the plate or could not hit to left or to right field

RUBE FOSTER'S CHICAGO AMERICAN GIANTS DOMINATED BLACK BASEBALL IN THE MIDWEST FOR OVER A DECADE.
Negro Leagues Baseball Museum, Inc.

RUBE FOSTER WAS AN ACCLAIMED PITCHER, OWNER OF THE
CHICAGO AMERICAN GIANTS, AND FOUNDER AND COMMISSIONER
OF THE FIRST NEGRO NATIONAL LEAGUE.
Negro Leagues Baseball Museum, Inc.

when ordered," remarked Frank A. Young, a well-known Chicago sports editor. Many of his players sprinted a hundred yards in less than ten seconds. They also considered bunting an essential skill. The speedy base running and the skillful bunting frequently paid off. In a game against the Indianapolis ABCs, the American Giants trailed at the end of the seventh inning by 18–0. Foster gave the bunt signal to eleven batters in a row. Two others hit grand-slam home runs. The American Giants had tied the score, 18–18, when darkness ended the game.

The fans loved this exciting ball playing, and they packed the stadium to see the American Giants. In popularity Foster's team rivaled Chicago's two major league teams, the Cubs and the White Sox. All three clubs played at home one Sunday; six thousand fans saw the Cubs, nine thousand saw the White Sox, and eleven thousand saw the American Giants.

Many blacks were seeing big league baseball for the first time. Between 1910 and 1920, the number of black people living in Chicago doubled to 110,000. Most of the newcomers had fled the South, where they had endured poverty and cruel treatment by white people. Although the North offered no escape from racism, it did offer plenty of factory and stockyard jobs. The fast-growing black population in Chicago and in other northern cities increased the number of baseball fans. The time was right, Foster decided, to create a league.

In February 1920, Foster and a group of black businessmen met at the Kansas City, Missouri, YMCA to organize the Negro National League. The original NNL consisted of the Chicago American Giants, Chicago Giants, St. Louis Giants, Dayton Marcos, Detroit Stars, Indianapolis ABCs, Kansas City Monarchs, and Cincinnati Cuban Stars.

Foster said he wanted "to create a profession that would

PROUD KANSAS CITY MONARCHS IN 1924. THE TEAM WAS
CREATED IN 1920 TO REPRESENT KANSAS CITY IN THE NEGRO
NATIONAL LEAGUE.
National Baseball Library, Cooperstown, N.Y.

equal the earning capacity of any other profession . . . keep
Colored baseball from the control of whites [and] do something
concrete for the loyalty of the Race." Like other influential
black leaders of the time, he believed that black people, largely
excluded from white society, should develop and depend on
their own businesses and organizations. Although he wanted
an all-black NNL from team owners to bat boys, Foster re-
luctantly accepted one white man into the league.

J. L. Wilkinson, owner of the newly formed Kansas City
Monarchs, had been a minor-league pitcher before becoming

owner and manager of the All Nations, a barnstorming team with a lineup that included blacks, whites, and Asians. Despite Foster's apprehensions, Wilkinson proved extremely popular and successful. "He was one white man who was a prince of a fellow," a Monarchs player once commented. "He loved baseball and he loved his players." This devotion combined with skillful managing to make the Monarchs one of black baseball's leading teams.

Wilkinson and the other club owners elected Foster NNL commissioner. Foster became a tireless, selfless booster of the league. "Foster's whole heart and soul," Frank Young felt, "was wrapped up in the game." He raised money to organize the Detroit Stars and sent Pete Hill, a prized player and manager, to coach the new franchise. Foster also returned Oscar

A PASS SIGNED BY J.L. WILKINSON, THE WHITE MAN WHO OWNED THE KANSAS CITY MONARCHS, PROBABLY BLACK BASEBALL'S MOST FAMOUS TEAM
Larry Lester and Negro Leagues Baseball Museum, Inc.

Charleston, the star outfielder who had joined the Giants a couple of years earlier, to the Indianapolis ABCs to strengthen that Indiana club.

The NNL inspired the organization in the spring of 1920 of the Southern Negro League. This new league included the Atlanta Black Crackers, New Orleans Crescent Stars, Memphis Red Sox, Birmingham Black Barons, and Nashville Elite Giants. The SNL was a poor cousin to the NNL. The northerners often snapped up the southern league's better players, such as first baseman George "Mule" Suttles, outfielder Norman "Turkey" Stearnes, and pitcher Satchel Paige.

Foster's American Giants initially dominated the NNL. They won the league pennant in 1920, 1921, and 1922. At the end of the season, the NNL champions challenged the top eastern teams to an unofficial black world series.

The American Giants in 1922 faced the Atlantic City Bacharach Giants in Chicago. They dueled nineteen innings with neither team scoring. Then the Bacharachs made a fatal mistake. They put Ramiro Ramirez in right field. Ramirez, Foster noticed, had a weak arm. With Cristóbal Torrienti on second, Foster signaled his batter to hit to right field. The batter popped the ball just over the first baseman's head. The right fielder quickly snared the ball. As the runner rounded third, Ramirez threw toward home plate, but the throw fell short. Torrienti slid into home and the American Giants beat the Bacharachs 1–0.

The official Negro World Series began in 1924, a year after East Coast teams organized the Eastern Colored League. The ECL charter members were Philadelphia's Hilldale Club, Brooklyn Royal Giants, Atlantic City Bacharach Giants, New York Lincoln Giants, New York's Havana Cuban Stars, and Baltimore Black Sox. The Hilldale Club and the Kansas City

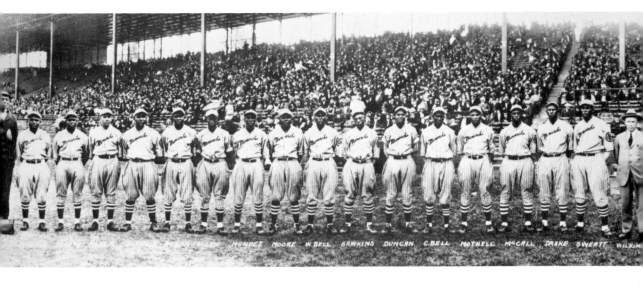

THE KANSAS CITY MONARCHS BEFORE THE START OF THE
EIGHTH GAME OF THE FIRST NEGRO WORLD SERIES
National Baseball Library, Cooperstown, N.Y.

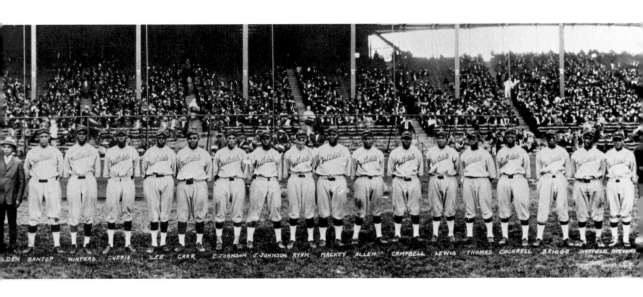

PHILADELPHIA'S HILLDALE CLUB BEFORE THE START OF THE
EIGHTH GAME OF THE FIRST NEGRO WORLD SERIES
National Baseball Library, Cooperstown, N.Y.

Monarchs met in the first Negro World Series. The two pennant winners played nine games in front of forty-five thousand fans in four different cities, Philadelphia, Baltimore, Kansas City, and Chicago.

With the series split four games apiece, the teams faced off in Chicago for the last game. It remained scoreless until the bottom of the eighth, when Kansas City exploded. Five hits, a walk, a sacrifice, and great base running put the Monarchs ahead 5–0. They held Hilldale in the last inning and became the first World's Colored Champions. The winning pitcher, a thirty-seven-year-old Cuban named José Méndez, pitched a two-hit shutout.

Hilldale avenged itself in the next nine-game Negro World Series by winning five of the first six games against Kansas City. The American Giants won the following two Negro World Series, both years defeating the Bacharachs. Tragically, Rube Foster did not see his team triumph in either Negro World Series.

In the middle of the 1926 season, Foster suffered a nervous breakdown. He spent the rest of his life in a hospital. The man had devoted a quarter of a century to baseball. Black people across the nation were immensely proud of the superb American Giants and of the professionally organized Negro National League. But even Foster's devotion had failed to stabilize the NNL, and without him the problems worsened.

Lack of money constantly troubled the league. Some teams could not afford to travel. Several dropped out of the league after only a season or two. In 1923, neither the Toledo Tigers nor the Milwaukee Bears, both new to the NNL that year, finished the season. Even the Negro World Series proved disappointing at the gate. For playing six games in the 1925 series, the winning Hilldale players received only twenty-five

FUTURE MONARCHS? A GROUP OF BOYS IN KANSAS CITY
INTERRUPT THEIR BASEBALL GAME TO POSE FOR A PHOTOGRAPH.
Janet Bruce Campbell

dollars each. As one disgruntled player remarked, "We could have made more in two games barnstorming than we'll get out of the whole series."

Black clubs depended on barnstorming to pay the bills. In the days before television, touring teams gave fans of all colors a chance to see exciting big league baseball. Whenever a barnstorming team came to town, local people declared a holiday and flocked to the ball field.

A POSTER PROMOTING A GAME BETWEEN A BARNSTORMING
BLACK TEAM AND A WHITE TEAM. BARNSTORMING TEAMS
CRISSCROSSED THE COUNTRYSIDE PLAYING COUNTLESS
SMALL-TIME CLUBS.
Refocus Films

5

BARNSTORMING

LIFE ON THE ROAD

It is a warm, yellow September Sunday in the late 1920s, barely noon, ordinarily a time when there is little motion in Pittsburg, Kansas. Today the town is in ferment. Broadway, the main street, streams with traffic, all bound north to the fairgrounds. The Fords, the Essexes, the Chevies, and Darts, the Buicks and Hupmobiles growl along, bumper to bumper, many bearing Missouri, Oklahoma, or Arkansas tags.

The pedestrian traffic swings along the walk thickly. Some fathers, carrying picnic baskets in one hand, support young sons on the opposite shoulder.

Then, abruptly at Fourth Street, the traffic breaks. A moment passes. Into the vacuum an army of boys and girls come sweeping and planing on their bikes, the vanguard for the Monarchs bus carrying the team. The players had dressed a block down the street at the Y with its showers and lockers, essential for all the fried chicken, hams, piccalilli, cakes, pies, and other edibles the townsmen will present through the day to the Monarchs.

This holiday scene, vividly recalled by an old newspaper reporter, occurred whenever a famous barnstorming team such as the Monarchs or the American Giants came to town to play the local club. People quit work early, prepared picnic lunches, and spent the day at the ballpark. The large crowds often spilled onto the outfield. Fans unable to squeeze into the park watched the game perched in nearby trees or on roof-tops.

During the summer and fall, barnstorming teams criss-crossed the countryside playing countless small-town clubs. When the weather turned cold and snowy, players headed to southern California, Florida, Cuba, or Mexico for winter base-ball. The following spring they meandered north, stopping in towns and cities along the way to challenge local teams.

Wherever they traveled, the Negro leaguers seldom failed to impress their fans. "I shall not forget the first time I saw Rube Foster," recalled a college student in New Orleans. "I never saw such a well-equipped ball club in my whole life. I was astounded. Every day they came out in a different set of beautiful uniforms, all kinds of bats and balls, all the best kinds of equipment." To this young man the life of a big league baseball player appeared very glamorous. And in many ways it was.

In an era when few people traveled, the big leaguers were men of the world. They frequently visited California and New York, faraway places to most people. These men regularly played in such foreign countries as Canada, Mexico, and Cuba. In 1927 an all-star black team sailed halfway around the world to Japan. They stopped along the way for games at exotic ports in Hawaii, the Philippines, Australia, and China.

The American Giants, the Kansas City Monarchs, and other successful black teams impressed fans because they

"TRAVELING THRU CANADA IN DR. YAK. I DROVE THIS THING ALL
OVER CANADA. OUR WHOLE TEAM WITH WILKIE." A PLAYER
SENT THIS PHOTOGRAPH AND MESSAGE HOME TO HIS FAMILY. DR. YAK
WAS THE CAR'S NICKNAME, AND WILKIE WAS J. L. WILKINSON,
THE POPULAR OWNER AND MANAGER OF THE MONARCHS. THE
TEAM AND ITS EQUIPMENT TRAVELED IN THIS CAR.
National Baseball Library, Cooperstown, N.Y.

traveled like business tycoons, presidents, and major league teams—by private Pullman coach. This luxurious train car was furnished with bunk beds and a galley kitchen, where a cook fixed the team's meals.

More commonly, teams toured by private bus or car. This enabled them to follow flexible schedules and visit smaller cities and towns not served by trains. The poorer clubs rode from game to game with as many as fourteen players and their equipment squeezed into two cars. Richer teams, like the Monarchs, crisscrossed the country in a "parlor bus" with a luggage rack on top and seats for twenty-one people. The

THE FEW HOTELS OR GUEST HOUSES WHERE BLACK BASEBALL
PLAYERS, OR ANY BLACK TRAVELERS, WERE WELCOME USUALLY
DISPLAYED "COLORED ONLY" SIGNS.
Schomburg Center for Research in Black Culture

Kansas City team occasionally took along tents and other
camping gear to sleep under the stars. The hardest part of
barnstorming for every black team was finding places to sleep
and eat.

"We couldn't stay in white hotels, we couldn't eat in restaurants," remembered one veteran barnstormer. "In cities
there were usually Negro hotels. In those small towns we
would stay in family houses, two players here, two players

there. Sometimes they'd fix us a meal in the colored church, or we'd bring out food from the grocery store in a paper sack. . . . In some of those small towns we couldn't stay, and sometimes we'd just ride all night and sleep in the bus. Then we'd have to play ball the next day. A lot of times we couldn't take a bath after the ball game. I remember once in Colby, Kansas, we set tubs of water out in the sun to get them warm so we could take a bath."

These men resented not being able to sleep in hotels or eat in restaurants, but only seldom could they protest. "One time in Elkhart, Indiana," another barnstorming veteran recalled, "we went in the restaurant and ordered some hamburgers, about thirty-six. The man had them on the grill. One of the fellows said, 'I'll just sit down and have a piece of pie and a glass of milk while I'm waiting.' The waitress said, 'I'm sorry we don't serve you like this, this is sack service.' We said, 'All right, since we can't eat here, you people have a good time eating all those hamburgers.' We walked out and left them on the grill."

Negro leaguers and major leaguers often barnstormed together, which proved very profitable for both sides. For playing in the 1946 World Series, Stan Musial, a well-known white first baseman, received only $4,000. Afterward, for playing several games against Satchel Paige, Musial received $10,000. Paige's reputation always guaranteed big crowds and good paychecks.

Paige, a skinny six-foot, three-inch pitcher, began his big-league career in Alabama in 1928 with the Birmingham Black Barons. For many years he threw only one pitch, a deadly accurate fastball. "He was the fastest I ever saw," recalled an opposing player. "He was so fast you couldn't bunt him. . . . it was nothing but fire." When Paige's fastball began slowing

DIZZY DEAN, MIDDLE, AND SATCHEL PAIGE, RIGHT, WERE TWO
OF THE TOP PITCHERS OF THE 1930S.
Negro Leagues Baseball Museum, Inc.

down in the late 1930s, he developed a curve, a slider, and a fadeaway.

The lanky pitcher's reputation rested both on his blazing fastball and showmanship. In some games, usually in the sixth or seventh inning against a weak opponent, Paige told his outfield to retire. In the remaining innings he would strike out every batter. Paige also enjoyed yelling—loud enough for everyone in the stands to hear—exactly what pitch he planned to throw next. The hapless batter, of course, did not stand a chance. By the time he began to swing, the ball had smacked the catcher's mitt. Fans loved these antics. They filled ballparks just to see Paige. Teams often hired the popular pitcher by the game. He would pitch only two or three innings in return for as much as 15 percent of the ticket sales. Paige retired when he was nearly fifty years old. By then he estimated that he had worn the uniforms of 250 different teams.

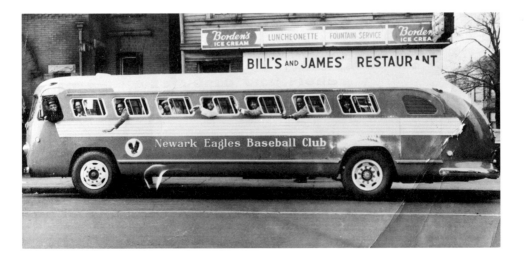

THE NEWARK EAGLES, ONE OF THE MORE PROSPEROUS NEGRO LEAGUE TEAMS, ON THEIR WAY TO A GAME
Refocus Films

SATCHEL PAIGE AND HIS BARNSTORMING TEAM IN 1946
Refocus Films

Paige frequently competed against such legendary major leaguers as Babe Ruth, Dizzy Dean, and Bob Feller. Paige and Dean last faced each other in 1942. At age thirty Dean had just retired from major league baseball. In eight years in the majors, the right-handed pitcher led the National League in strikeouts four seasons. The Homestead Grays, with thirty-six-year-old Paige pitching for one game, faced Dean and his all-star squad in front of thirty thousand fans in Griffith Stadium in Washington, D.C. Paige and the Grays thrashed Dean and his all-star team 8–1. Dean, now in the Hall of Fame, considered Paige one of the greatest pitchers of all time. "My fastball," he once remarked, "looks like a change of pace alongside that pistol bullet old Satch shoots up to the plate."

Bob Feller, another Hall of Fame pitcher, joined Paige in 1946 for one of the last big barnstorming tours between an all-black team and an all-white team. Few people then traveled by air, but the two pitchers chartered airplanes and flew their teams from city to city. In twenty-six days, they played thirty-two games before four hundred thousand people.

Many black teams also barnstormed in Cuba, Mexico, and Puerto Rico, where they developed a special relationship with the people and the players of these countries.

6

BÉISBOL

THE CUBAN CONTRIBUTION

If you could pitch and win down there," declared one pitcher, "you could pitch and win anywhere." "Down there" was Cuba, the big Caribbean island just ninety miles south of Florida. The Cubans loved baseball and played the game year round. In late fall many American teams, both major league and Negro league, sailed to that island for exhibition games. Black players frequently joined the local teams, and many Cubans played in the Negro leagues.

One of the best Cuban Negro leaguers was José Méndez, the pitcher who won the ninth and crucial game of the first Negro World Series in 1924. Méndez was a highly regarded player in the United States, but he was a national hero in Cuba. In the 1908–9 season, pitching for the Almendares Blues, Méndez had a 15–6 record. He led the Cuban league in victories, completed games, and shutouts. For five more seasons the young man led the league in both wins and shutouts. The pitcher also faced thirty-eight visiting major and minor

FROM LEFT TO RIGHT, PABLO MESA, OSCAR CHARLESTON, AND
ALEJANDRO OHMS PLAYING FOR SANTA CLARA IN CUBA
National Baseball Library, Cooperstown, N.Y.

league clubs from the United States, winning twenty-five of those games. Méndez played his first summer in the United States in 1909. He pitched forty-six games for the Cuban Stars and won all but two.

While the Negro leagues recruited dark-skinned Cubans, the major leagues recruited light-skinned Cubans. The Cincinnati Reds in 1911 signed two of Méndez's Almendares teammates, Rafael Almeida and Armando Marsans. These were the first Cubans in the twentieth century to play in the majors. Another Cuban teammate, pitcher Adolfo Luque, was the National League's leading pitcher in 1923, with a 27–8 record for the Cincinnati Reds. But fewer Cubans played in the major leagues than in the Negro leagues. And the Cuban Negro leaguers were among the island's most talented athletes.

The Pittsburgh *Courier*, one of the nation's foremost black newspapers, in 1952 picked an all-time, all-star Negro league team. It included Cristóbal Torrienti. The newspaper praised the outfielder's "deceptive speed and the ability to cover worlds of territory, from the right-field foul line to deep right center. He was one of the best ball hitters in baseball." Torrienti, born in Havana in 1895, achieved stardom by age twenty. In 1916, he batted .402 and led the Cuban league in triples, home runs, and stolen bases. He joined the Chicago American Giants in 1918 and consistently batted in the high .300s. He led the entire NNL in 1923, batting .389.

The most outstanding Cuban in the Negro leagues was Martín Dihigo. New York Giants manager John McGraw called him a great, natural baseball player. Mexican fans called him El Maestro, and Cuban fans El Immortal. Dihigo was born in 1905 in Matanzas, Cuba. At age seventeen he joined the Havana Reds. The following year, 1923, the teenager toured the United States with New York's Havana Cuban Stars.

PITCHER ADOLFO LUQUE, ONE OF THE FIRST CUBANS TO PLAY
IN THE MAJOR LEAGUES. HE WAS THE NATIONAL LEAGUE'S
LEADING PITCHER IN 1923.
National Baseball Library, Cooperstown, N.Y.

Despite poor hitting he impressed observers. "The best youngster to come off the island since pitcher José Méndez," declared one sportswriter. "He fields like a veteran and has good speed but has not learned how to hit the curve ball." Dihigo improved his hitting, and in Cuba three seasons later batted .421.

Dihigo played only a few years in the United States, but in a short time he made a big impression. After three seasons

MARTÍN DIHIGO, AN ALL-ROUND CUBAN PLAYER, WAS ELECTED
TO THE NATIONAL BASEBALL HALL OF FAME IN 1977.
*Morgan and Marvin Smith and Schomburg Center for Research in
Black Culture*

in Venezuela, Dihigo in 1935 joined the New York Cubans. He batted .323 that year and tied Josh Gibson as the league's leading home run hitter. Dihigo played every position except catcher. On the mound his record was 6–2. During his last season in the United States, Dihigo topped the league in batting with an average of .393 and again tied Gibson for the lead in home runs.

Dihigo played for another nine years in Cuba and in Mexico, where he pitched for the Aguila team of Veracruz. In 1938, attractive salaries lured Josh Gibson, Willie Wells, and other black baseball stars to Mexico. Despite the tougher competition, Dihigo led the Mexican league in games won, strikeouts, and batting. In the playoffs Aguila faced Agrario, a club from Mexico City. Dihigo knocked a ninth-inning home run that clinched the playoffs, two games to one. That same season, the Cuban hurled the Mexican league's first no hitter. El Maestro finished the year with a remarkable 18–2 record, 184 strikeouts, and a .387 batting average.

After Dihigo retired in the mid-1940s, a newspaper editor reported that the baseball legend frequently entertained his many admirers in Havana's open air cafés. "The name Dihigo was like saying Mr. Baseball. It was like saying Babe Ruth.

THE NEW YORK CUBANS, A NEGRO LEAGUE TEAM IN THE 1930S AND 1940S, FIELDED BOTH CUBANS AND AMERICAN BLACKS.
Schomburg Center for Research in Black Culture

A GAME IN SANTO DOMINGO, DOMINICAN REPUBLIC, IN 1940
Luis Munoz

He'd sit and give lectures about baseball, and people would sit there in awe and listen." Even after retirement Dihigo set another record. He was elected to four baseball halls of fame: in Cuba, Mexico, Venezuela, and the United States.

People in Cuba and in other Spanish-speaking countries adored the visiting black American baseball stars. They showed that affection by giving the Americans nicknames. Willie Wells was El Diablito, or the little devil. The shortstop was such an amazing fielder, people joked, that he must have had the devil's help. John Henry Lloyd was Cuchara, or the scoop, because of his big hands, which scooped up grounders. Fans showed their appreciation in other ways too. When one man hit a crucial home run, Cuban fans "went wild with joy and gave him a case of beer, a box of cigars, a shirt and tie, money, and a barbecued pig."

Negro leaguers enjoyed playing in these countries because they were treated better than they were at home in America. "I remember one trip we made from Philadelphia to Havana," recalled Max Manning, a Newark Eagles pitcher. "We got on the train in Philadelphia, and we had to stay in a colored-only compartment. We couldn't even leave to get some food. When we finally arrived in Cuba, we were treated as heroes. We could stay at any hotel, eat at any restaurant."

Baseball's popularity spread from the United States and

A BASEBALL CARD OF PUERTO RICO'S TEAM GUAYAMA. IT INCLUDES SATCHEL PAIGE AND, IN THE CENTER, TETELO VARGAS, THE GREAT DOMINICAN OUTFIELDER.
Luis Munoz

Cuba to other countries around the Caribbean. In 1934 Josh Gibson and a group of Negro leaguers toured Puerto Rico. Soon afterward Puerto Rican players formed their first league. It consisted of five teams: San Juan, Aguadilla, Caguas, Ponce, and Santurce.

The Caribbean and Latin countries frequently lured American athletes to their ball clubs with irresistibly high salaries. In 1937, Rafael Trujillo, the Dominican Republic dictator, raided the Pittsburgh Crawfords. He paid nine of the team's star players $30,000 to join his team. A few years later, Mexican millionaires lured other top Negro league players south. Some, such as Josh Gibson, ended their careers in Mexico. But most returned to the United States and to the uncertain fortunes of the Negro leagues.

7

SURVIVING THE 1930s

HARD TIMES TO GOOD TIMES

On a cold, rainy December Sunday in 1930, three thousand quiet mourners huddled in the rain outside St. Mark's Methodist Episcopal Church at Fiftieth and Wabash Avenue in Chicago. "BASEBALL'S GREATEST FIGURE DEAD," lamented a bold, front-page newspaper headline. Rube Foster had died. It was a sad day for his family and friends and for fans throughout the country.

Many people thought Foster's death also meant the death of the Negro leagues. Their decline had begun two years earlier, when the Eastern Colored League, its teams squabbling over schedules and gate receipts, collapsed. Since there was no ECL, there was no Negro World Series. The NNL, without Foster, had become so disorganized and unprofitable that the Monarchs dropped out to barnstorm the entire season.

Other events added to the league's problems. In 1929 the stock market collapsed, real estate values plummeted, thousands of businesses went bankrupt, and banks, afraid of running out of money, locked their doors. The Great Depression, one of the most serious crises in the nation's history, gripped the land. One fourth of the country's workers were jobless. People could barely afford to eat, so they were not spending money to see ball games. This was particularly true in black communities, where even in good economic times most people earned very little money. To survive, the black clubs needed new ways to attract fans.

The most enduring idea to come out of depression-era baseball was the night game. There had been many baseball games under artificial lights since Thomas Edison patented his version of the electric lamp in 1879, but the Kansas City Monarchs were the first to use lights regularly.

In 1929, the Monarchs spent $50,000 on a portable lighting system. It consisted of several trucks, each one supporting two poles that held six floodlights. The poles, raised by derricks, telescoped forty-five feet into the air. A 250-horsepower motor ran a generator that supplied electricity for the lights. The noisy motor and generator, nearly the size of an automobile, sat in center field. Its cables snaked across the grass to the lights positioned around the diamond. When chasing fly balls, the outfielders kept glancing at the ground to avoid tripping over the thick cables.

Night games boosted attendance tremendously. The first games under the lights drew as many as twelve thousand spectators. "When one considers the fact that really good Sunday games usually attract only about three thousand," a writer observed, "it can be said with some accuracy that the night ball idea has caught the fancy of the fans." The Cincinnati Reds, in 1935, were the first major league team to install lights.

The creation of a new Negro National League gave black

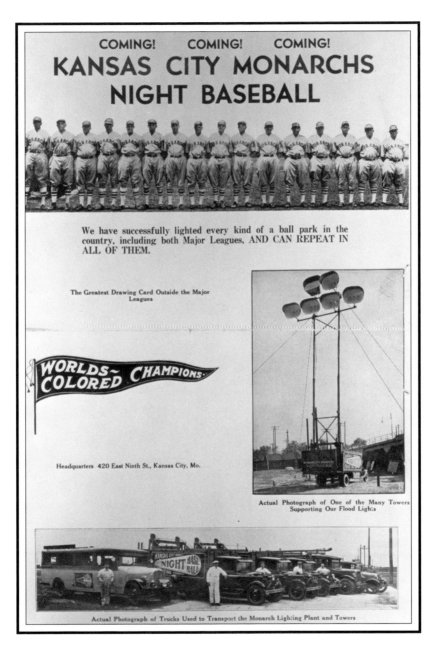

THIS MONARCHS POSTER USED THE NOVELTY OF NIGHT
BASEBALL TO PROMOTE GAMES.
National Baseball Library, Cooperstown, N.Y.

baseball another boost. Soon after Rube Foster's death, his league died, the victim of poor leadership and the Great Depression. Gus Greenlee, a wealthy black gambler from Pittsburgh, came to the rescue. He launched the annual East-West All-Star Classic in 1933. That year he also organized a new Negro National League. The league consisted of seven teams: the Philadelphia Stars, Nashville Elite Giants, Newark Eagles, New York Cubans, New York Black Yankees, the Homestead Grays, and Greenlee's own team, the Pittsburgh Crawfords.

The Crawfords were sensational. The 1935 lineup included Oscar Charleston, Judy Johnson, Cool Papa Bell, Satchel Paige, and Josh Gibson. All five men are enshrined in the National Baseball Hall of Fame at Cooperstown. Judy Johnson,

THE NEW YORK BLACK YANKEES, SHOWN HERE IN 1939, WERE ONE OF NEW YORK CITY'S TOP TEAMS.
Morgan and Marvin Smith and Schomburg Center for Research in Black Culture

the sixth Negro leaguer inducted into the Hall, played third base for the Crawfords. He stood five feet, eleven inches and weighed only 150 pounds. A strong right-handed batter despite his light weight, Johnson compiled a career average of .303.

In regular season play, the Crawfords attracted as many as two hundred thousand fans. This popular team survived only until 1938, a year after its top players deserted Pittsburgh to play in the Dominican Republic. Afterward, Green-

FIRST BASEMAN BUCK LEONARD, WHO JOINED THE HOMESTEAD GRAYS IN 1924, STRETCHES TO SNAG A HIGH THROW. LEONARD WAS ONE OF THE HIGHEST PAID PLAYERS IN THE NEGRO LEAGUES.
Schomburg Center for Research in Black Culture

THE 1935 PITTSBURGH CRAWFORDS, CHAMPIONS OF THE NEGRO
NATIONAL LEAGUE, INCLUDED FIVE FUTURE HALL OF FAME
MEMBERS. THEY WERE OSCAR CHARLESTON, ON THE LEFT,
SATCHEL PAIGE, SECOND FROM THE RIGHT, JOSH GIBSON,
FOURTH FROM THE RIGHT, COOL PAPA BELL, SEVENTH FROM
THE RIGHT, AND JUDY JOHNSON, EIGHTH FROM THE RIGHT.
Schomburg Center for Research in Black Culture

lee's influence in baseball declined. But the Crawfords, the NNL, and the East-West games all contributed to the growing respect for black athletes.

A year after the first East-West All-Star Classic, the *Denver Post* Tournament invited the Kansas City Monarchs to compete against the country's top Triple-A teams. They were

THIRD BASEMAN JUDY JOHNSON PLAYED FOR HILLDALE AND FOR THE PITTSBURGH CRAWFORDS. HIS EXCEPTIONAL FIELDING AND BATTING EARNED HIM A SPOT IN THE NATIONAL BASEBALL HALL OF FAME IN 1975.
Negro Leagues Baseball Museum, Inc.

THE DENVER POST

C. L. (POSS) PARSONS, SPORTS EDITOR

Roar of Crowd Was Sweet Music to Their Ears

DIZ CARRITHERS.   HUGHES OF NEGRO ALL-STARS SAFE AT THIRD.

SATCHEL PAIGE.   MOOSE PINKERTON.   FRANK WARREN.   BUZZ ROSS.

Stars of Sunday's games received big ovations from the overflow crowd. Diz Carrithers and Satchel Paige pitched superbly in winning their games. Warren and Ross of Huber Carbon Co. of Borger, Tex., helped make it easy for Carrithers with their heavy hitting. Pinkerton hit a long homerun over the right-field fence, but even that couldn't put Lexington, Neb., in the game with Borger.

AT A TIME WHEN FEW PHOTOGRAPHS OF BLACK PEOPLE
APPEARED IN DAILY NEWSPAPERS, COLORADO'S LARGEST
NEWSPAPER FEATURED THE STARS, WHITE AND BLACK, OF THE
DENVER POST TOURNAMENT.
Refocus Films

the first blacks ever invited to that popular Colorado tournament. One newspaper called the invitation "the most significant announcement of a decade to the extent that Negro baseball was concerned." The Monarchs finished second that year, but the following year they won the tournament and the $7,500 first prize.

Blacks were also prominent in the National Baseball Congress Tournament in Wichita, Kansas. In 1935, the tournament's first year, a team of white and black players sponsored by a Bismarck, North Dakota, automobile salesman captured the $10,000 first prize. The Bismarck squad included Satchel Paige, Quincy Trouppe, and Hilton Smith. Impressed by Trouppe, one major league scout exclaimed that the catcher would be worth "$100,000 if he were white."

Hilton Smith was a better pitcher, some people believed, than the more famous Paige. In two Wichita tournaments, Smith pitched and won five games. In 1937, in his first appearance as a Kansas City Monarch, Smith hurled a perfect game against the American Giants. Later that year he threw another perfect game against Bob Feller and a team of major league all stars. Smith pitched eleven years for Kansas City and compiled an enviable record of 161–22.

At the beginning of the 1930s, black baseball was in disarray. By the end of that decade, with exciting games and large crowds, new Negro leagues were beginning to rival the major leagues in popularity. More people began noticing the terrific black players.

8

RUMORS

WHO WOULD BE THE FIRST BLACK MAJOR LEAGUER?

There's a couple of million dollars' worth of baseball talent on the loose . . . yet unsigned by any major league," observed a *Washington Post* sportswriter in 1939. "There are pitchers who would win twenty games this season for any big-league club that offered them the contracts, and there are outfielders who could hit .350, and infielders who could win quick recognition as stars."

Ever since segregation began, major league coaches had been glancing enviously across the color line at the great black players. By the 1940s more was afoot than wishful looks.

During World War II, which America entered in late 1941, the military drafted many major league players. The men left in the game were either too young, too old, or otherwise unfit for service. Eighteen Cincinnati Reds were classified by their draft boards as 4-F, or physically unsuitable for military duty. Major league teams were desperate for players. One team recruited a boy in junior high school. Another signed a one-armed outfielder, who batted .200 in 1945. Junior high school and one-armed players only emphasized the desperation of major league baseball. Fewer and fewer fans came out for the games.

At the same time attendance at Negro league games soared. The draft took blacks too, but Negro leaguers often began their careers as teenagers and played until their forties. Although many black players were either too young or too old for the draft, they were exciting to watch on the ball field. "Those days during the war, Negro baseball was drawing more fans than it ever did," Satchel Paige wrote in his autobiography. "Everybody had money and everybody was looking for entertainment and they found plenty in Negro baseball. Even the white folks was coming out big."

A record number of fans—51,723—turned out for the 1943 East-West All-Star Classic to cheer such legends as Paige, Cool Papa Bell, Josh Gibson, and Buck Leonard. The all stars represented the decade's outstanding teams—the Monarchs, the Baltimore Elites, the Newark Eagles, and the powerhouse of the day, the Homestead Grays.

From 1937 until 1945, the Grays won the Negro National League pennant eight times. The team originally represented Homestead, Pennsylvania, a steel-mill town near Pittsburgh. In the late 1930s, the Grays began scheduling Saturday games in Pittsburgh and Sunday games in Washington, D.C. In both cities the black team played in major league stadiums, providing an important source of income for the stadium owners. The Pennsylvania team, outdrawing the lackluster Washington Senators, often attracted thirty thousand fans to their games in the nation's capital.

The Grays biggest stars were catcher Josh Gibson and first baseman Buck Leonard. When fans discuss the Negro

MANY PEOPLE THOUGHT JOSH GIBSON, A SUPERB CATCHER
AND POWERFUL SLUGGER, WOULD BE THE FIRST BLACK PLAYER
IN THE MODERN MAJOR LEAGUES.
Refocus Films

league's most outstanding black players, Gibson is mentioned frequently. Existing records show that he batted .526 in 1943. In ten East-West games, he batted .483. Against Gibson, one opposing pitcher said, "You threw the ball and prayed." A Washington Senators pitcher exclaimed: "There is a catcher that any big-league club would like to buy for $200,000. . . . He can do anything. He hits the ball a mile. And he catches so easy he might as well be in a rocking chair. Throws like a rifle."

Buck Leonard, the other half of this famous duo, began his professional career at age twenty-five, after losing his job as a railroad porter. The solidly built left-hander stood nearly six feet and weighed 185 pounds. He excelled at first base and consistently batted in the high .300s. Leonard's career lasted twenty-three years, ending in Mexico in the mid-1950s.

Leonard, Gibson, and Paige were the three highest paid players in black baseball. Paige in the early 1940s reportedly earned $37,000 a year. The famous pitcher boasted that "the majors couldn't pay me enough" to switch leagues because he

ALTHOUGH HE WAS ONE OF THE VERY BEST PLAYERS IN THE NEGRO LEAGUES, SCOUTS CONSIDERED BUCK LEONARD TOO OLD FOR THE MAJORS. HE RETIRED IN 1955 AT AGE FORTY-EIGHT.
Negro Leagues Baseball Museum, Inc.

already earned four times more than the average major leaguer. In 1971, Paige became the first Negro league player chosen for the National Baseball Hall of Fame. Both Leonard and
Gibson were inducted into the Hall of Fame in 1972.

Black baseball became the mirror image of the major
leagues in 1937, when team owners organized the Negro
American League. The NAL included the Kansas City Monarchs, the Birmingham Black Barons, Chicago American Giants, Cincinnati Clowns, Cleveland Buckeyes, and the
Memphis Red Sox. The NNL and NAL revived the Negro
World Series five years later. The 1942 series pitted the Grays
against the Monarchs. Led by ace pitchers Satchel Paige and
Hilton Smith, the Monarchs swept the first four games in that
best-of-seven-game series.

As Negro league players such as Paige and Gibson became
widely known, the black press began publishing stories about
integrating the major leagues. Black people—especially in the
northern cities, where they had been migrating for decades—
had more political and economic power than ever before. The
war against racist Nazi Germany also changed white attitudes
about segregation. People no longer assumed that blacks
would never play in the majors. Instead, they asked who
would be the first? The possibilities abounded.

In 1942, all-round college athlete Jackie Robinson tried out
for the Chicago White Sox. As a student at the University of
California at Los Angeles, Robinson excelled in four sports:
track, baseball, basketball, and football. In his junior and senior years, he led his basketball conference in scoring. Senior
year he was a football all-American. Baseball, people said, was
Robinson's worst sport. But he impressed the White Sox.
"He's worth $50,000 of anybody's money," the team's man-
ager remarked after the tryout. "He stole everything but my
infielders' gloves."

The following year the Pittsburgh Pirates were scouting Roy Campanella. The young catcher began his professional career with the Baltimore Elites in 1936 when he was a fifteen-year-old high school student. He was a squat five feet, nine inches and weighed some two hundred pounds. By the 1940s, he was a seasoned catcher, admired for his strong, accurate throws to second and for his powerful hitting. "We were all in on scouting Campanella," recalled a Dodger official. "You couldn't go wrong there."

The Washington Senators, desperately needing help out of the American League cellar, asked Leonard and Gibson if they would join the team. "Of course," the two men said. "Well," replied the owner, "nobody wants to be the first to take blacks in the major leagues. But we know you boys can play ball. You boys can play good baseball, and some of us would like to have you."

Bill Veeck, a white manager who had long admired the talented men in black baseball, planned the boldest strategy of all. He would buy the Philadelphia Phillies, who were near last place in the National League. Then he would recruit Satchel Paige, Josh Gibson, Willie Wells, and others. "The only untapped reservoir of players were some of the blacks who were either older or for one reason or another had not been drafted," Veeck explained. "I had not the slightest doubt that in 1944, a war year, the Phils would have leaped from seventh place to the pennant." He made the mistake of explaining his plan to the commissioner of baseball, Kenesaw Mountain Landis. The commissioner did not like Veeck's plan. He ordered the Phillies sold to another buyer.

Many people thought Landis, who had been baseball's iron-fisted commissioner since 1921, was the main obstacle to integration. That opposition ended in 1944, when Landis died. The new commissioner, Albert B. "Happy" Chandler, a U.S.

TERRIS McDUFFIE TRIED OUT
FOR THE BROOKLYN DODGERS IN 1945.
National Baseball Library, Cooperstown, N.Y.

Senator from Kentucky, said he did not object to blacks in the majors. "If they can fight and die on Okinawa, Guadalcanal, in the South Pacific," he stated, mentioning two of the fiercest battles of World War II, "they can play baseball in America." Was he serious? No one knew. But many people were eager to find out.

On a cool April day in 1945, David "Showboat" Thomas and Terris McDuffie arrived uninvited and unannounced at the Brooklyn Dodgers spring training camp. Both men were Ne-

ROY CAMPANELLA BEGAN HIS PROFESSIONAL CAREER AT AGE
FIFTEEN AS A CATCHER FOR THE BALTIMORE ELITE GIANTS.
Refocus Films

JACKIE ROBINSON WITH HIS NEW BOSS, BROOKLYN DODGERS
MANAGER BRANCH RICKEY
Refocus Films

gro league standouts. Thomas, considered the best black first baseman in America, played for the New York Cuban Giants. McDuffie was a leading pitcher for the Newark Eagles. The Dodgers management grudgingly agreed to give the two men a tryout. For an hour Thomas fielded and batted while McDuffie threw to a Dodger catcher. But the Dodgers already had other plans to recruit blacks, so they never seriously considered either player.

Only a week later, three Negro leaguers tried out for the Boston Red Sox. They were Sam Jethroe, an outfielder with the Cleveland Buckeyes who had led the NNL in hitting in 1942 and 1944; Marvin Williams, a Philadelphia Stars second baseman hitting .338 that season; and Jackie Robinson, by then a Kansas City Monarchs rookie.

Recalling the tryout, Jethroe said: "I wasn't nervous. None of us were. We were just out there doing a job because we all thought we were very good. We didn't feel all that bad about it. I remember Cronin [one of the coaches] telling us that we all had the ability to play in the big leagues, but that blacks simply weren't being allowed at that time."

More indignantly, Robinson recalled: "We knew we were wasting our time. Nobody was serious then about black players in the majors." Robinson, of course, did not know that soon he would be the first.

In late 1945, the Brooklyn Dodgers made headlines by signing Jackie Robinson to their farm team in Montreal, Canada. After a sensational season with Montreal, the young athlete made headlines again in 1947 by moving up to the Brooklyn Dodgers. Sportswriters dubbed Robinson's entry into the majors "the great experiment." The experiment worked better than anybody ever dreamed.

9

SUPERSTARS

THE FIRST BLACKS IN THE MAJORS

Jackie's nimble / Jackie's quick / Jackie's making the turn-stiles click." So rhymed a Pittsburgh *Courier* sportswriter, delighted that Robinson's exciting style of playing was filling ballparks.

Robinson played the game as Rube Foster and other Negro leaguers had played. Few major leaguers in those days bunted. But Robinson excelled at bunting and at base stealing. In his first season Robinson bunted forty-six times, for an exceptional fourteen hits and twenty-eight sacrifices. Once on base he kept the fielders on their toes. In one game, Robinson was on second and the score was tied with one out. The batter popped up to center field for an easy second out. When the fielder caught the ball, Robinson tagged up and dashed to third. On the next pitch the catcher missed the ball. As the fans jumped to their feet cheering wildly, Robinson raced home to score and put the Dodgers ahead.

Robinson did indeed make the turnstiles click during his first major league season. Over forty-six thousand people, a

JACKIE ROBINSON STEALS HOME! ROBINSON'S DARING BASE
RUNNING KEPT FANS ON THEIR FEET.
UPI/Bettmann

stadium record, filled Chicago's Wrigley Field two hours before a game between the Dodgers and the Cubs. When Robinson first played in St. Louis, Memphis blacks chartered a train to that Missouri city to see their hero. Thousands of adoring fans joined Jackie Robinson clubs. One writer dubbed Robinson the "headline man" because newspapers and magazines published more articles and photographs of him than of any other sports figure. He became so famous that people have nearly forgotten the other Negro league players who joined the major leagues.

Eleven weeks after Robinson put on a Dodgers uniform, Larry Doby signed with the American League's Cleveland Indians. Bill Veeck bought the ailing Indians in 1946, and the following year began signing black players. Doby had been a prominent New Jersey high school athlete who had won all-state honors in basketball, baseball, and football. After serving in the navy during World War II, Doby played his first full professional season in 1946 with the Newark Eagles. He played second base and batted .339 that year, the fourth highest in the Negro National League.

During his first season at Cleveland, Doby warmed the bench. The following year Veeck put Doby into the lineup as an outfielder. He started slowly, batting less than .200. But then, in just four games, his average jumped 50 percent. Against the Washington Senators, he slugged a high fly that soared four hundred feet over center field. The ball struck a loudspeaker thirty-five feet above the fence and bounced onto the field and in play. Sliding head first, Doby barely beat the throw to home plate for a rare inside-the-park home run. The next game, hitting three singles and a 440-foot home run, he scored three times and batted in two runs. Doby ended the 1948 season batting .301.

That year, for the first time in the memory of many Cleve-

LARRY DOBY, SLIDING HOME, WAS ANOTHER YOUNG STAR FOR
THE NEWARK EAGLES. HE WAS THE FIRST BLACK RECRUITED
BY THE AMERICAN LEAGUE.
Schomburg Center for Research in Black Culture

land fans, the Indians were in the race for the pennant. It had been twenty-eight years since the team last won a pennant. Veeck asked forty-two-year-old Satchel Paige to try out for the team. "I couldn't help but be impressed by his uncanny ability to throw the ball where he wanted," the Indians manager recalled. "Satch was in the strike zone four out of every five pitches." Veeck paid the Negro league star a full year's salary to pitch the last three months of the season. He was the first black to pitch in the American League. Paige started in twenty-one games, won six, lost one, and helped Cleveland win the pennant.

SATCHEL PAIGE, ON THE LEFT, WITH BILL VEECK, MANAGER
OF THE CLEVELAND INDIANS
Negro Leagues Baseball Museum, Inc.

Doby's hitting, Paige's popularity, and the close pennant race brought out the fans. Attendance at Indians games jumped to 2,600,000 that season, a million more fans than the previous year. The Cleveland Indians set baseball attendance records for a single game, a night game, a season, and a World Series game. In the fourth game of the World Series against the Boston Braves, with the Indians trailing two games to one, Doby slugged a home run that clenched that decisive game. Cleveland went on to win the series four games to two.

That same year Roy Campanella broke into the major leagues. The Brooklyn Dodgers recruited the young catcher in early 1946, only a few months after signing Robinson. Campanella played two seasons in the minors before the Dodgers brought him up. Campanella was Most Valuable Player in 1951, 1953, and 1955. He hit forty-one home runs in 1953, a record among catchers. At the end of the season Campanella was named Outstanding National League Player.

The year after Campanella moved to Brooklyn, thirty-one-year-old Monte Irvin joined the Dodgers crosstown rival, the New York Giants. Many people had expected Irvin to be the first black to break into the major leagues. As a high school student in New Jersey, he had been all-state in football, baseball, basketball, and track. The University of Michigan offered him an athletic scholarship, but he lacked the money to make

MONTE IRVIN, A NEWARK EAGLES STAR, JOINED THE NEW YORK GIANTS.
National Baseball Library, Cooperstown, N.Y.

RAY DANDRIDGE, ANOTHER FORMER NEWARK EAGLE, CROSSING
HOME PLATE AFTER HITTING A HOMER FOR THE MINNEAPOLIS
MILLERS. IN 1987, HE WAS THE LAST NEGRO LEAGUER
SELECTED FOR THE HALL OF FAME.
National Baseball Library, Cooperstown, N.Y.

the long trip to the Midwest. He attended a Pennsylvania college for a year before dropping out to play shortstop for the Newark Eagles from 1939 to 1942.

The Eagles, owned and managed by civil rights activist Effa Manley, was a major team in the last years of Negro league baseball. Its lineup included Leon Day and Ray Dandridge. Many people feel that Day, a pitcher with a tremendous fastball and a high strikeout average, deserves recognition in Cooperstown. Dandridge, on the other hand, was the last Negro league player chosen for the Hall of Fame. In 1949 the New York Giants signed the thirty-five-year-old third baseman to its Minneapolis Millers farm team. In four

THESE THREE NEW YORK GIANTS, FROM LEFT TO RIGHT,
MONTE IRVIN, WILLIE MAYS, AND HANK THOMPSON, WERE
MAJOR LEAGUE BASEBALL'S FIRST ALL-BLACK OUTFIELD.
UPI/Bettmann

seasons at Minneapolis, Dandridge batted over .300 and was named Rookie of the Year and Most Valuable Player. This exceptional performance, combined with his outstanding Negro league record, earned Dandridge a plaque in the Baseball Hall of Fame in 1987.

Irvin, at age thirty, also left the Newark Eagles for the New York Giants in 1949. He and outfielder Hank Thompson, a young second baseman from the Kansas City Monarchs, were the first blacks in the Giants lineup. These two men, along with another famous black player, helped create the miracle finish of 1951.

Willie Mays was the third member of that trio. Like Cam-

WHEN MAJOR LEAGUE TEAMS BEGAN RECRUITING BLACK
PLAYERS, THOUSANDS OF BLACK PEOPLE BEGAN ATTENDING
GAMES. HERE, WILLIE MAYS GREETS HIS FANS.
Layne's Photo and Schomburg Center for Research in Black Culture

panella, Mays began playing professional baseball in high
school, as an outfielder for the Birmingham Black Barons. The
New York Giants signed the young man in 1950. They sent
him to Minneapolis, where he performed phenomenally. His
second season in the minors, Mays batted .607 in the first
fourteen games and .477 after thirty-five games. In mid-season
the Giants called Mays to New York. He joined Irvin and
Thompson to form an all-black outfield. Led by those three

men, the Giants came from thirteen and one-half games behind to win the National League pennant.

Mays was Rookie of the Year in 1951, beginning one of the most outstanding careers in major league baseball. He led the National League in home runs four different years and, with 660 homers, ranks third behind Henry Aaron and Babe Ruth in career home runs. He was named Baseball's Player of the Decade for 1960–9.

While a handful of black players became superstars and millions of black fans rejoiced in the integration of major league baseball, it was a sad time for the Negro leagues. The white teams took their best young players, and black fans began attending major league games. "Today Negro baseball finds itself flat on its back," lamented one writer in the late 1940s, "attempting to rise after suffering a knockout blow."

Attendance at Newark Eagle games dropped from 120,000 in 1946 to 57,000 in 1947, to a dismal 35,000 the following year. A group of Texas businessmen bought the Eagles and moved the team to Houston. At the end of the 1948 season, both the Homestead Grays and the New York Black Yankees went out of business. And the venerable old man of baseball, J. L. Wilkinson, who had helped organize the first Negro National League back in 1920, sold the Kansas City Monarchs and retired from baseball. The NNL folded in 1948, and five years later only four teams remained in the NAL.

After Robinson joined the Dodgers, the annual East-West All-Star Classics initially drew larger crowds because fans hoped to see future major league stars. The 1945 East-West game attracted fewer than thirty-eight thousand fans, but the 1946 game drew over forty-five thousand. And in 1947 attendance topped forty-eight thousand. Then, people lost interest, and by 1953 the last of the dream games had become sleepy events, attended by fewer than ten thousand people.

FORMER NEGRO LEAGUER COOL PAPA BELL WITH FORMER
MAJOR LEAGUERS MICKEY MANTLE AND WHITEY FORD AND
NATIONAL LEAGUE UMPIRE JOHN CONLAN AT THEIR INDUCTION
IN 1974 INTO THE NATIONAL BASEBALL HALL OF FAME
National Baseball Library, Cooperstown, N.Y.

EXTRA INNINGS

Most of the men in the Negro leagues did not have a chance to play in the major leagues. As the number of black teams dwindled, former players hung up their cleats and found other jobs. They became school teachers, barbers, janitors, mail carriers, and night watchmen. For many years, few people seemed to remember or to care that these men once had been among the greatest black athletes in America. But that is changing.

In August of 1991, seventy-five former players, many bent and gray from their years, met in Cooperstown, New York. They were attending the first Negro league reunion at the National Baseball Hall of Fame. At a banquet in their honor, the commissioner of baseball praised the men's long years of unselfish devotion to the game. For three days they laughed and joked and reminisced about those years of glory.

The old players, many for the first time, saw the Negro league exhibit in the Hall of Fame Museum. The photographs of Oscar Charleston, Satchel Paige, and Josh Gibson evoked smiles and tears as the memories came rushing back: the long, tiring bus rides while barnstorming from game to game, the festive mood in the small towns as people crowded around for autographs and close looks at the big league players, and the spine-tingling thrill of being greeted by fifty thousand roaring fans at an East-West All-Star Classic.

Sadness too tinged the reunion. "I have mixed feelings," remarked one old player as he stared at a giant photograph of the 1935 Pittsburgh Crawfords kneeling in front of their team bus. "This is a little late in life, don't you think? A lot of my friends up there didn't live to see this." Most of the players at the reunion had never visited Cooperstown, said Buck O'Neil, a former Kansas City Monarch, and most would never return.

While all of the old Negro leaguers will be gone some day, their place in history will be remembered, thanks to the work of several organizations. A special selections committee studies the existing Negro leagues records and recommends players for the Hall of Fame. In 1971 the Hall inducted its first Negro leaguer, Satchel Paige. Since then the Hall of Fame has inducted ten more Negro league players. They are Josh Gibson, Buck Leonard, Monte Irvin, Cool Papa Bell, Judy Johnson, Oscar Charleston, John Henry Lloyd, Martín Dihigo, Rube Foster, and Ray Dandridge. These men, unlike Jackie Robinson and Willie Mays, who are also in the Hall of Fame, played most of their careers in the Negro leagues. According to Buck O'Neil, at least twelve other Negro leaguers should be in the Hall of Fame. But these players are prevented from entering the Cooperstown pantheon because the official records of their accomplishments are incomplete.

The Negro League Committee of the Society of American

Baseball Research is working to complete the record. The committee is a nationwide network of volunteers busily digging into old newspapers and other records of the past to provide complete team and player statistics. Because of their efforts, baseball encyclopedias now publish Negro league statistics.

One of the most significant tributes to black baseball is the Negro Leagues Baseball Museum in Kansas City. When construction of a new building is finished, the museum's exhibits and films will tell the story of the Negro league to current and future generations.

For over half a century, black baseball lifted spirits and gave hope to millions of black people throughout segregated America. Those bittersweet years should never be forgotten.

ADDITIONAL SOURCES
OF INFORMATION ON THE
NEGRO LEAGUES

National Baseball Hall of Fame and Museum
P.O. Box 590
Cooperstown, NY 13326

A permanent exhibit devoted to the Negro leagues is in the Hall of Fame Museum. The exhibit includes photographs, gloves, bats, and other equipment donated by players. The Hall of Fame Library maintains a Negro leagues file of newspaper clippings, magazine articles, and other information. The photographic archive has numerous photographs of teams and players. Copies are available for a fee. The museum's gift shop sells Negro league baseball caps and uniforms.

Negro Leagues Baseball Museum
1601 East 18th Street
Suite 206
Kansas City, MO 64108

The museum maintains photographic and research archives. Copies of photographs are available for a fee. The museum also sells copies of Negro league posters and other memorabilia.

Society for American Baseball Research
P.O. Box 93183
Cleveland, OH 44101

SABRE's Negro League Committee is a nationwide network devoted to research and to sharing information. The committee publishes a newsletter and keeps files of newspaper and magazine articles on the Negro leagues. Members frequently publish articles on the Negro leagues in SABRE publications.

GLOSSARY

All-state A term describing high school athletes who are chosen as among the best within their home state in a particular sport.

Barnstorm A barnstorming baseball team traveled from town to town, stopping only long enough to play a game against a local team. The two teams shared the money fans paid for admission.

Batting average The number of base hits a player has made compared to the number of times at bat. The higher the number, the better the hitter. An average of .300 is very good. It means that the batter got a hit three out of every ten times at bat. Walks and sacrifices are not included in the average.

Bunt When a batter taps the baseball so that it rolls only a few yards from home plate. The bunt is frequently used to advance runners already on base.

Cellar A sports expression that means last place.

Fadeaway The old name for a screwball. This pitch both spins and curves. The fadeaway, or screwball, breaks right for a right-handed pitcher and breaks left for a left-handed pitcher. This is the opposite of a curve ball.

Farm team   A minor league team owned by a major league club. Players are assigned to farm teams to develop the skill needed for major league baseball. Branch Rickey, when he was manager of the St. Louis Cardinals, created the farm team system.

International league   One of the first minor leagues. It was organized in the late nineteenth century and included teams from the United States and Canada.

Inside-the-park homerun   While most homeruns are hit into the stands, an inside-the-park homerun is usually hit deep into the outfield. This kind of homerun is rare because the ball is usually fielded and thrown home faster than the batter can run the bases.

Perfect game   When none of the twenty-seven batters a pitcher faces during the nine innings of a game gets on base.

Power hitter   An unusually good batter.

Slider   A fastball that breaks slightly in the same direction as a curve. Curves thrown by right-handed pitchers break left, and curves thrown by left-handed pitchers break right.

Triple A   Minor league teams are rated Single A, Double A, and Triple A. The rating indicates the quality of the team. Triple A is the best.

Win-loss record   For example, the unusually good record of 105–17 means the team won 105 games while losing only 17 games. The number of games won always appears first.

FURTHER READING

Adler, David A. *Jackie Robinson: He Was the First.* New York: Holiday House, 1990.

Brashler, Williams. *Josh Gibson: A Life in the Negro Leagues.* New York: Harper & Row, 1978.

Bruce, Janet. *The Kansas City Monarchs: Champions of Black Baseball.* Lawrence: University Press of Kansas, 1985.

Campanella, Roy. *It's Good To Be Alive.* New York: Signet, 1974.

Einstein, Charles. *Willie's Time: A Memoir of Another America.* New York: Berkley Books, 1980.

Grabowski, John. *Jackie Robinson.* New York: Chelsea House Publishers, 1991.

_____. *Willie Mays.* New York: Chelsea House Publishers, 1990.

Holway, John B. *Black Diamonds: Life in the Negro Leagues from the Men Who Lived It.* Westport, Conn.: Meckler Books, 1989.

_____. *Blackball Stars: Negro League Pioneers.* Westport, Conn.: Meckler Books, 1988.

_____. *Voices from the Great Black Baseball Leagues.* New York: Dodd, Mead, 1975.

Humphrey, Kathryn Long. *Satchel Paige.* New York: Watts, 1988.

Macht, Norm. *Satchel Paige*. New York: Chelsea House Publishers, 1991.

Mays, Willie with Lou Sahadi. *Say Hey: The Autobiography of Willie Mays*. New York: Simon & Schuster, 1988.

Moore, Joseph Thomas. *Pride Against Prejudice: The Biography of Larry Doby*. New York: Praeger, 1988.

O'Conner, Jim. *Jackie Robinson and the Story of All-Black Baseball*. New York: Random House, 1989.

Paige, Leroy "Satchel" and David Lipman. *Maybe I'll Pitch Forever*. New York: Doubleday, 1962.

Peterson, Robert. *Only the Ball Was White*. New York: McGraw-Hill, 1984.

Robinson, Jackie. *Baseball Has Done It*. New York: Lippincott, 1964.

Robinson, Jackie and Alfred Duckett. *Breakthrough to the Big Leagues*. New York: Harper & Row, 1965.

———. *I Never Had It Made*. New York: Fawcett, Crest, 1974.

Rogosin, Donn. *Invisible Men: Life in Baseball's Negro Leagues*. New York: Atheneum, 1983.

Ruck, Rob. *Sandlot Seasons: Sport in Black Pittsburgh*. Urbana: University of Illinois Press, 1987.

Scott, Richard. *Jackie Robinson*. New York: Chelsea House Publishers, 1987.

Seymour, Harold. *Baseball: The People's Game*. New York: Oxford University Press, 1990.

Trouppe, Quincy. *20 Years Too Soon*. Los Angeles: Sands Enterprises, 1977.

Tygiel, Jules. *Baseball's Great Experiment: Jackie Robinson and His Legacy*. New York: Oxford University Press, 1985.

Veeck, Bill. *Veeck as in Wreck: The Autobiography of Bill Veeck*. New York: Fireside, 1989.

INDEX

Page numbers in *italics* refer to photographs.

ABOUT THE AUTHOR

Michael L. Cooper has been a travel writer, publishing feature articles in Travel & Leisure, Outdoor Travel, The Washington Post, *and a variety of other publications. He is currently completing a Ph.D. in American history. This is his third nonfiction book for young readers. About it he says: "It was difficult to research because the record, both photographic and written, is so incomplete. Nevertheless, the Negro leagues lifted the spirits of and gave hope to countless black people throughout segregated America." Mr. Cooper lives in New York City.*